CONTENTS

Some of the projects in this book may require the use of craft knives, needles and pins. We would advise that young children are supervised by a responsible adult.

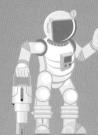

A SUIT FOR SPACE

An astronaut's space suit is covered in many bright badges. You can decorate yours with different designs. You will also need an **ID** badge!

To make and decorate your suit you will need:
A white sweatshirt
A pair of white trousers
Cardboard
Coloured paints and a paintbrush
Craft gems
Foam shapes
Craft glue and a paintbrush
A pair of scissors
A photo of yourself
Safety pins
White paper
Coloured tape and sticky tape
A ruler

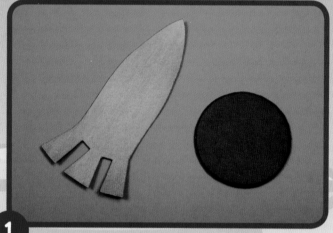

1 Cut out a circle and a rocket shape from cardboard and paint them bright colours.

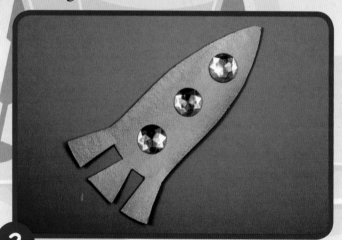

2 Glue gems down the middle of the rocket shape to look like windows.

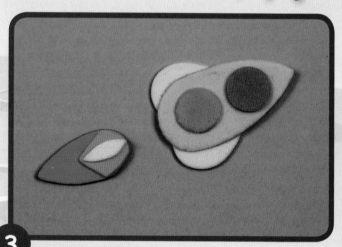

3 Make a space design out of foam shapes.

Glue a photograph of yourself onto your ID badge. With your space suit decorated you are well on the way to becoming a **space cadet!**

4 Glue the foam shapes to the card circle.

TIP:
You could write your name next to the photograph and make up your own astronaut ID number!

5 Cut a rectangle of cardboard that is 9 cm x 7 cm to make your ID badge. Cover with white paper. Stick coloured tape around the edges and decorate it. Leave a space to glue your photo in and draw some lines to write your name on.

6 Use sticky tape to attach safety pins to the back of your badges so that you can pin them to your sweatshirt.

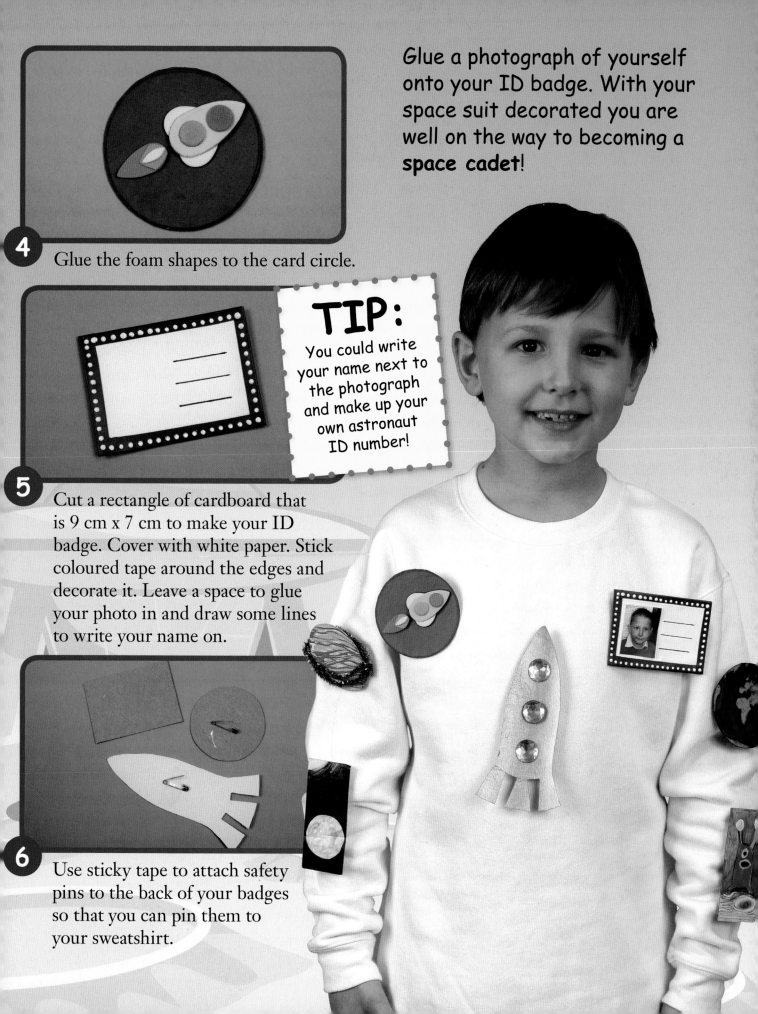

A HIGH-TECH HELMET

Astronauts need to wear protective helmets when they go into space. The helmet must be able to **survive** very hot and cold temperatures.

1 Measure around your head with a tape measure. Blow up a balloon so that it is slightly bigger than your head measurement.

2 Glue the newspaper strips to the top part of the balloon. Cover it with about three layers of newspaper.

3 When the glue is dry, burst the balloon and paint the dome white.

TIP:
If you want to make the glue runnier, mix four teaspoons of water with two tablespoons of craft glue in a jam jar.

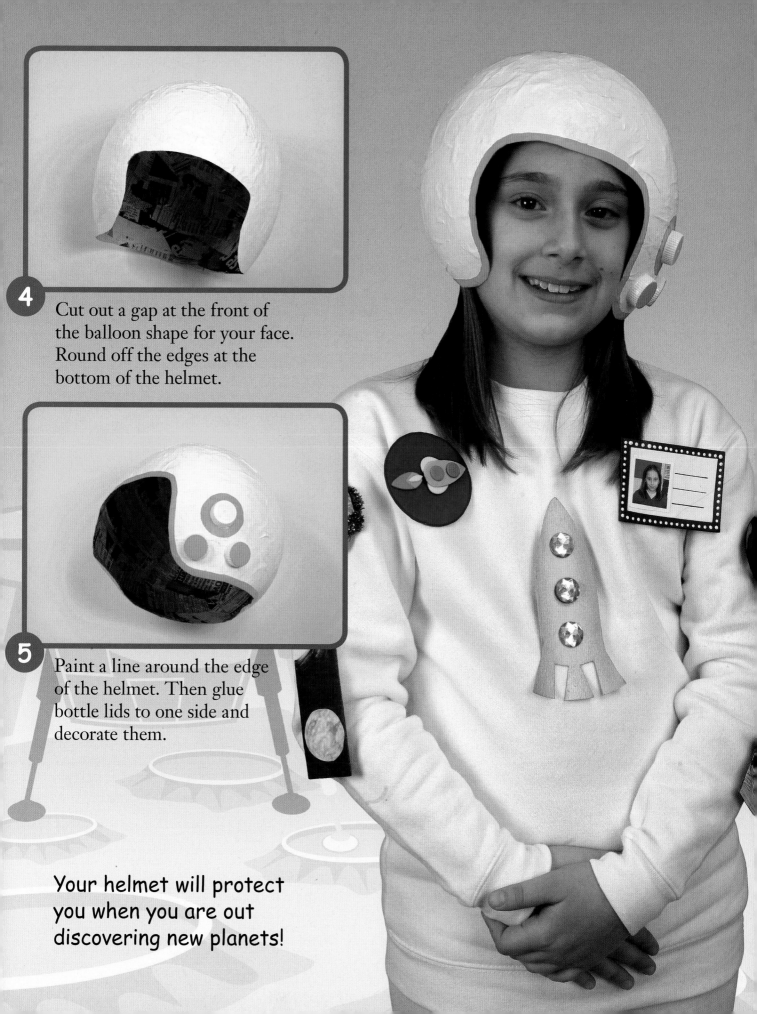

4 Cut out a gap at the front of the balloon shape for your face. Round off the edges at the bottom of the helmet.

5 Paint a line around the edge of the helmet. Then glue bottle lids to one side and decorate them.

Your helmet will protect you when you are out discovering new planets!

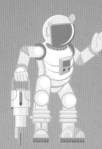

SPACE BOOTS AND EQUIPMENT BELT

An astronaut's job is to explore the **solar system**. Astronauts must wear special boots to walk on the surface of the planets. They need to wear a special belt to carry all of their equipment, too.

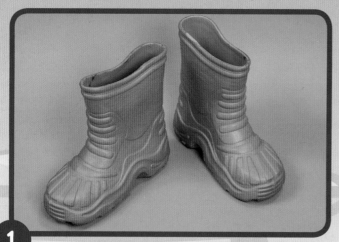

1 Paint the boots with metallic paint. You may need a few coats of paint.

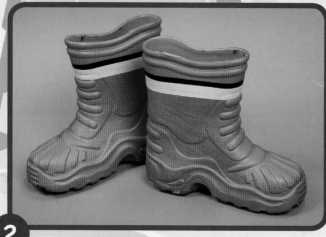

2 Stick coloured tape around the top of the boots.

3 Measure your waist with a tape measure. Cut a strip of elastic or stretchy fabric that is 3 cm longer than your waist measurement.

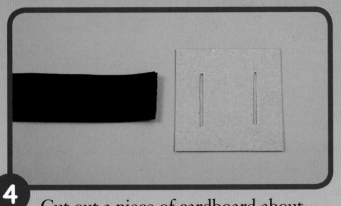

You are almost ready to set out on your journey to explore new worlds. You can add all sorts of space equipment to your belt!

4 Cut out a piece of cardboard about 8 cm square. To make the buckle, cut two slits in the cardboard using a craft knife. The slits should be about 2 cm from each side and be as long as the width of the elastic you are using for your belt.

5 Glue silver foil onto the cardboard buckle. When the glue is dry, cut through the slits. Decorate the buckle with coloured foam squares.

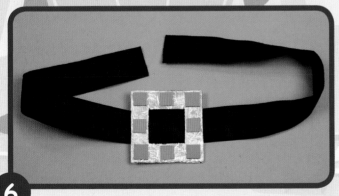

6 Thread the elastic through the buckle and glue a small piece of Velcro to each end so you can fasten your belt.

9

GATHERING MOON DUST

Astronauts collect **samples** from the planets to send to scientists back on Earth. They need to wear special gloves to protect their hands.

To make your space gloves and sample jars you will need:

Small, empty jam jars

Glitter, cotton wool, craft pompoms, beads

Sticky labels

A ruler

Bubble wrap

White paint and a paintbrush

Four plastic bottle tops

Sequins

Craft glue and a paintbrush

A pair of scissors

White cotton gloves

Coloured paints and a paintbrush

Coloured pens or pencils

Velcro

1 Fill the jam jars with brightly coloured things such as beads and glitter, or craft pompoms and cotton wool balls. Paint the lids different colours.

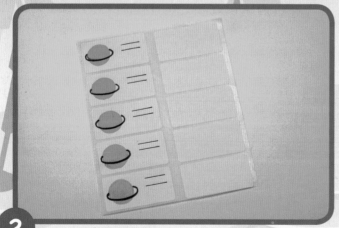

2 Design a **logo** and draw it onto the sticky labels. Draw lines with a ruler on the labels so you can write which planet your samples came from.

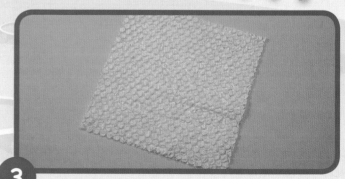

3 Cut out two pieces of bubble wrap about 24 cm square. Paint them white.

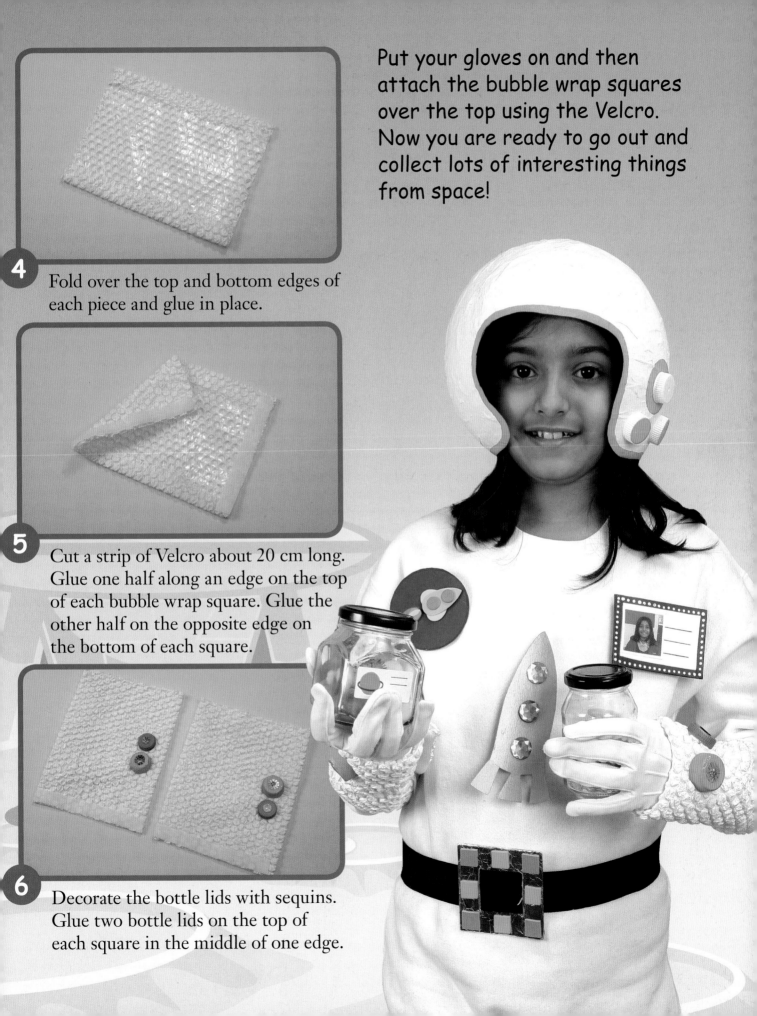

Put your gloves on and then attach the bubble wrap squares over the top using the Velcro. Now you are ready to go out and collect lots of interesting things from space!

4 Fold over the top and bottom edges of each piece and glue in place.

5 Cut a strip of Velcro about 20 cm long. Glue one half along an edge on the top of each bubble wrap square. Glue the other half on the opposite edge on the bottom of each square.

6 Decorate the bottle lids with sequins. Glue two bottle lids on the top of each square in the middle of one edge.

ASTRO PACK

Astronauts carry space packs on their backs. A space pack contains **oxygen** to help them breathe on other planets.

Make a space pack using:
Coloured electrical tape
2 large empty plastic bottles
A large cereal packet
100-cm length of clear plastic pipe
Paint and a paintbrush
100-cm length of white elastic
Newspaper, torn into strips
Sticky tape
Craft glue and a paintbrush
Foam shapes
A pair of scissors

1 Attach the bottles either side of the cereal packet using sticky tape.

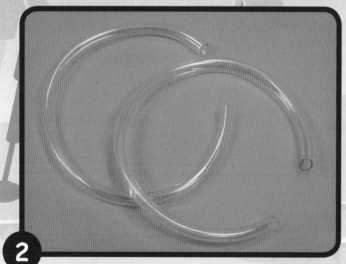

2 Cut the plastic pipe in half so that you have two 50-cm lengths.

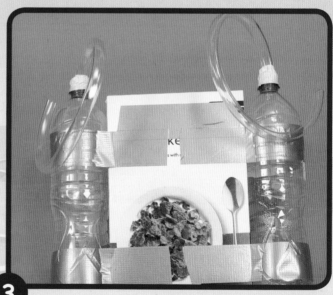

3 Insert one end of each pipe into the necks of the bottles. Use sticky tape to secure the pipes.

4 Make holes in the back of the cereal packet and push the other ends of the pipes into them.

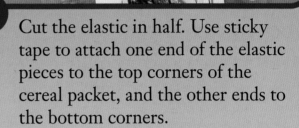

5 Cut the elastic in half. Use sticky tape to attach one end of the elastic pieces to the top corners of the cereal packet, and the other ends to the bottom corners.

TIP: If you want to make the glue runnier, mix four teaspoons of water with two tablespoons of craft glue in a jam jar.

6 Cover the packet and bottles in four layers of newspaper strips and glue.

Now you are ready to step out onto strange new planets. Beware of aliens!

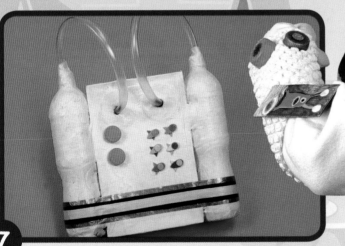

7 Paint the space pack and decorate it with coloured tape and foam shapes.

SPACE SPEAK

When astronauts are exploring planets they need to talk with their spaceship and also with scientists on Earth. They need a space radio to do this.

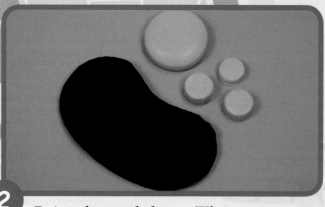

1 Draw two bean shapes on cardboard and cut them out. Glue them together and then cover them with strips of newspaper and glue. Continue until your space radio is nice and sturdy.

2 Paint the card shape. Then paint a jar lid and three bottle lids a different colour.

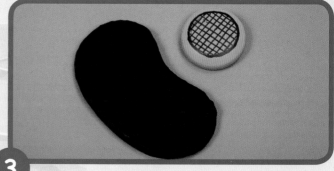

3 Use a permanent marker pen to draw lines across the jar lid from side to side and then from top to bottom. This will make a criss-cross pattern.

4

Glue the other bottle lids to the bean shape. Decorate with sequins.

5

Paint a polystyrene ball to match your bottle lids. Glue it to the end of a straw. Then glue the straw to the side of the bean shape.

6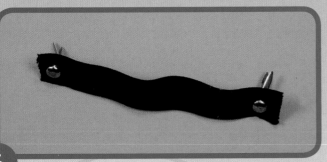

Cut a piece of elastic that is 2 cm wider than the middle of your space radio. Ask an adult to push split pins through the elastic around 1 cm from each end.

7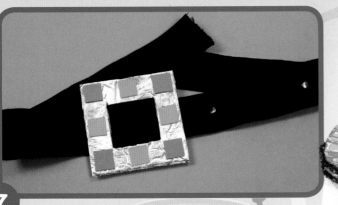

Push the split pin through your tool belt and open it. You can now tuck your space radio into your tool belt.

Now you can talk to your fellow astronauts wherever you are in space!

ALIEN LIFE DETECTOR

When an astronaut lands on another planet, one of the first things he needs to do is see if anything lives there. This alien life detector will do the job.

Make your detector using:
A 35-cm length of dowel
Coloured card
Coloured tape
Two polystyrene balls
A metallic pipe cleaner
Craft glue and a paintbrush
A pair of scissors
A biro
A compass
A pencil
A ruler
Coloured paint and a paintbrush

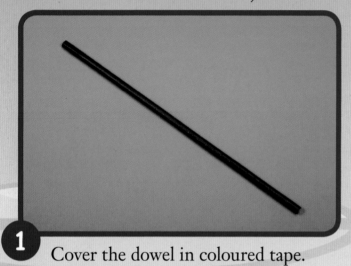

1 Cover the dowel in coloured tape.

TIP:
You could use a compass to draw the circles.

2 Draw six circles onto coloured card and cut them out. Make a hole in each one by pushing a biro through the middle.

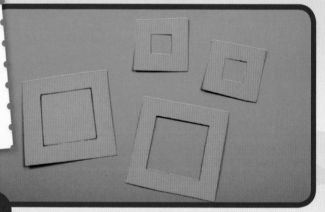

3 Draw two 12-cm squares and two 10-cm squares onto coloured card. Cut the squares out. Then draw a smaller square inside each one and cut them out, too.

4 Push the circles onto the dowel. Then glue the two pairs of squares together either side of the dowel.

5 Paint two polystyrene balls and glue them to the top and bottom of your stick. Then attach a metallic pipe cleaner to the squares at the top.

Now you are ready to go out and look for aliens of all shapes and sizes!

DO YOU BELIEVE IN ALIENS?

If you find a friendly alien, you might keep it with you as a pet.

1 Use scissors to carefully snip two small slits on each side of the toe end of the sock. Push a green pipe cleaner through the slits.

Make your own alien friend using:
A green sock
Two green pipe cleaners
Two polystyrene balls
Stuffing or old pairs of tights
Craft glue and a paintbrush
A plastic eye
Paint and a paintbrush
A pair of scissors

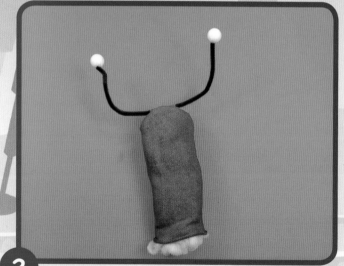

2 Push a polystyrene ball onto each end of the pipe cleaner. Stuff the sock with stuffing or pairs of tights.

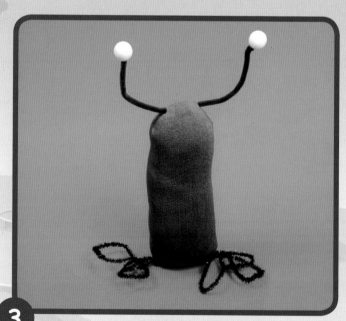

3 Place a pipe cleaner across the open end of the sock and glue the gap up. Bend the pipe cleaner to make feet shapes.

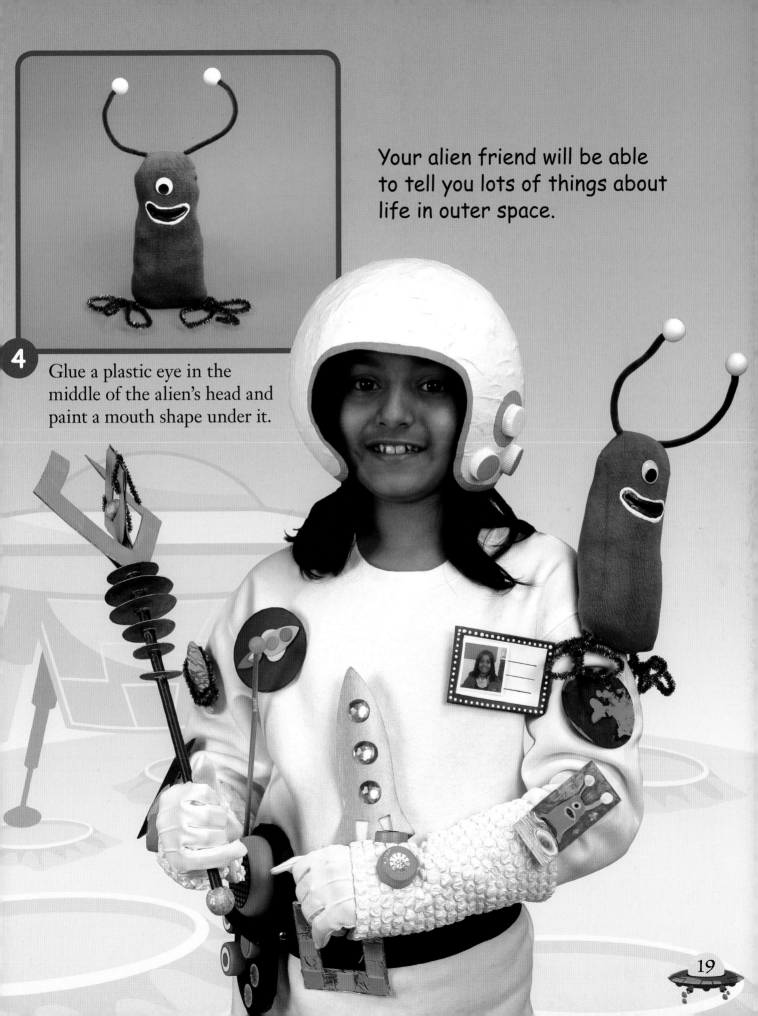

4 Glue a plastic eye in the middle of the alien's head and paint a mouth shape under it.

Your alien friend will be able to tell you lots of things about life in outer space.

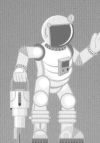

SNAPPING IN SPACE

Astronauts need a high-tech camera to photograph and video what they see in space.

1 Cover the cardboard box with foil. Cut a strip of coloured card and glue it around the edge of the box.

TIP:
You could draw a space picture or print out a photograph from the Internet.

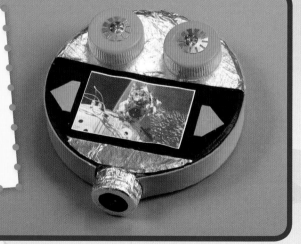

2 Glue a strip of black paper to the top of the box. Glue a space picture to the strip. Cut two small arrows out of coloured card and glue them either side of the picture.

3 Decorate three bottle lids with sequins. Glue two of them to the top of the box. Glue the other to the edge for the lens.

4 Cut a piece of elastic 2 cm longer than the width of the camera. Ask an adult to use split pins to attach the elastic to your tool belt. Then you can add the camera to your belt.

Now you can show everyone back on Earth the amazing sights you have seen!

FLY THE FLAG

Astronauts use flags to mark the places that they have visited in the universe. You could put your name or initials on your flag so people know what a great explorer you are!

1 Cut several circles out of coloured felt.

TIP: Make sure that you leave a gap of about 3 cm at the open end of your pillowcase.

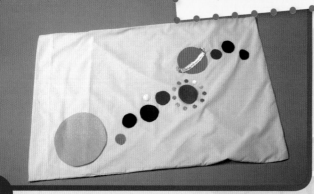

2 Glue the circles to the pillowcase. Add some foiled paper rings and sequins.

3 Draw some stars and other space shapes on foiled paper. Cut them out and glue them to the pillowcase.

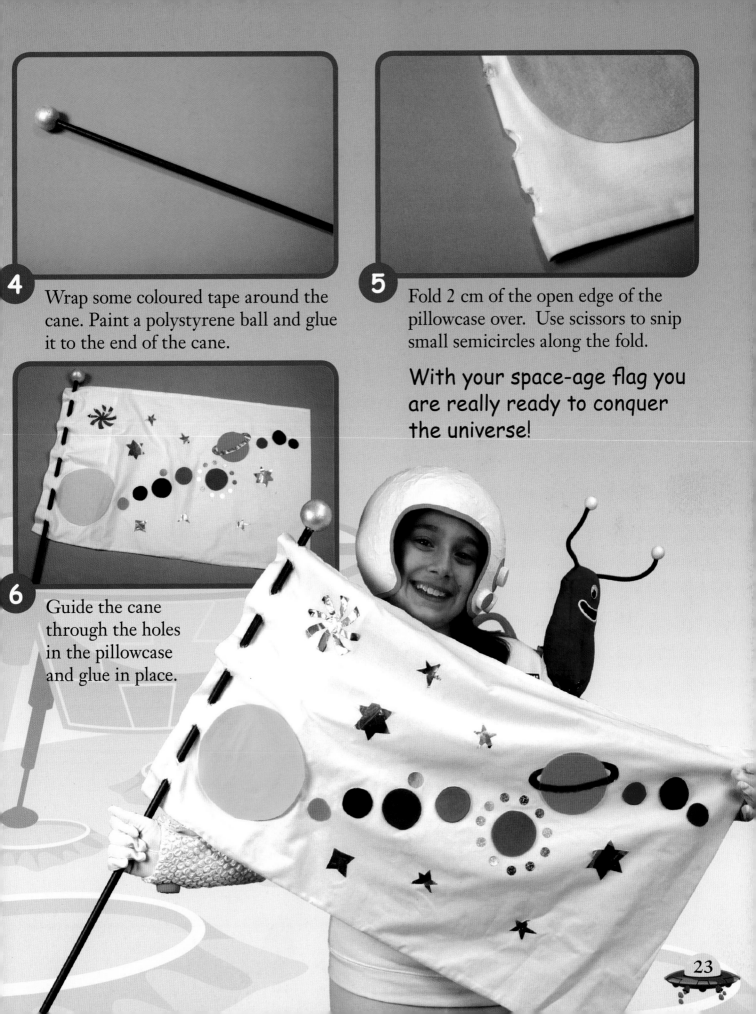

4 Wrap some coloured tape around the cane. Paint a polystyrene ball and glue it to the end of the cane.

5 Fold 2 cm of the open edge of the pillowcase over. Use scissors to snip small semicircles along the fold.

With your space-age flag you are really ready to conquer the universe!

6 Guide the cane through the holes in the pillowcase and glue in place.

GLOSSARY

ID stands for identification, which tells someone who you are
logo a design used by an organization
oxygen a gas that we need to breathe
polystyrene a white, foam-like material
sample a small amount of something used as an example
solar system the Sun and all the planets that surround it
space cadet someone who is training to be an astronaut
survive to be strong enough

FURTHER INFORMATION

Space – Sun, Moon and Stars by Sally Hewitt (Franklin Watts, 2008)
Astronaut (321 Go!) by Stephen Rickard (Ransom Publishing, 2010)
Astronauts Working in Space, First Facts, by Angela Royston (First Facts Books, 2010)

http://kids.msfc.nasa.gov/
A wide range of images, videos and interactive features from America's space agency.
Get the latest updates on NASA missions and even track the international space station.
www.kidsites.com/sites-edu/space.htm
A site with loads of interesting information about space. Learn about rockets, stars,
how a space station is built and how astronauts live in space.
www.esa.int/esaKIDSen
Would you like to be a real astronaut? This site can set you on the right track.

INDEX